This book belongs to:

Other magical books in the Enid Blyton collection

Enid Blyton's

The NEW Adventures of the Wishing~Chair

Winter Wonderland

Illustrated by Erica-Jane Waters

EGMONT

Special thanks to Narinder Dhami

EGMONT
We bring stories to life

The New Adventures of the Wishing-Chair: Winter Wonderland
first published in Great Britain 2009
by Egmont UK Limited
239 Kensington High Street
London W8 6SA

Text and illustrations ENID BLYTON® copyright © 2009
Chorion Rights Limited. All rights reserved.
Illustrations by Erica-Jane Waters

The moral rights of the author and illustrator have been asserted

ISBN 978 1 4052 4392 6

3 5 7 9 10 8 6 4 2

www.egmont.co.uk

A CIP catalogue record for this title is available from the British
Library

Printed and bound in Great Britain by Clays Ltd, St Ives plc

Contents

The Characters

Jack

Jessica

Wishler

Santa

Snowy

Coney

Reindeer

Chapter One

Jack was in bed, but he was far too excited to sleep. It was Christmas Eve. He snuggled under the duvet, wondering when Santa Claus would arrive with his reindeer.

Suddenly, Jack saw the bedroom

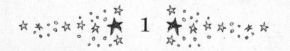

door open a crack.

'Jack, are you asleep?' Jessica whispered.

'Are you joking?' Jack sat up and switched on his bedside lamp. 'I'm waiting for Santa!'

'I was thinking . . .' Jessica slipped into the room in her dressing-gown. 'It's a bit mean to leave Wishler all

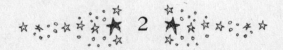

alone on Christmas Eve.'

'Let's go and visit him!' Jack suggested, jumping out of bed.

Wishler the pixie was Jack and Jessica's secret friend. He lived in the shed at the bottom of their garden, along with the magical wishing-chair that took the three of them on amazing adventures.

Jack put on his dressing-gown and

slippers and tiptoed behind Jessica

downstairs into the

kitchen. Jessica

wrapped up

some of the

star-shaped

cookies

that she

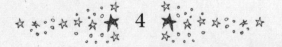

and Jack had baked for Santa while Jack unlocked the back door as quietly as he could.

'It's cold, isn't it?' Jack whispered as they went down the path to the shed. 'I wonder if it'll snow.'

'A white Christmas would be so lovely,' Jessica said.

Jack tapped on the shed door and

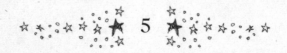

it swung open. Wishler stood there, a smile beaming all over his little pixie face.

'How wonderful to see you!' he exclaimed, ushering them into the warm, cosy shed.

'This is for you,' Jessica said, handing Wishler the package.

He unwrapped it and gave a cry of

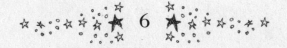

delight. 'Yummy!' he said, grinning widely.

A lamp glowed in the corner, lighting up the sparkling snowflake decorations that Wishler had put up and the beautiful, colourful

 7

paintings that covered the wooden

wishing-chair.

'The shed looks great, Wishler,'

Jack remarked.

'Your snowflakes are gorgeous, but

I wish we could have *real* snow,'

Jessica sighed. 'It just doesn't feel

like Christmas without it.'

'Hey, I've had a great idea,' Jack

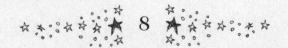 8

announced, bounding over to the wishing-chair. 'Maybe the chair could take us to a magical, snowy land.'

Wishler laughed. 'Well . . . Winter Wonderland has lots of snow,' he replied. 'And elves too. Even Santa Claus lives there.'

'Santa Claus!' Jack's eyes opened wide in amazement. 'You mean, we

can actually go and *meet* Santa?'

'Hmm . . .' Wishler scratched his head, looking doubtful. 'Maybe not. This *is* his busiest night of the year –'

'Look!' Jessica broke in. 'The paintings on the wishing-chair are changing.'

Jack and Jessica knew that whenever this happened, the chair

was ready to take them on a new

adventure. Now pictures of elves,

snowy pine trees, and colourfully

wrapped presents were appearing.

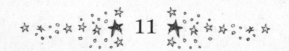

'The wishing-chair wants to take us to Winter Wonderland,' Wishler announced.

'Let's go right away!' Jack sat down on the chair, his face alight with excitement, and Jessica and Wishler joined him.

The three friends began to rock to and fro, and immediately bright

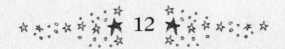

blue sparks began to flash round the

wishing-chair's rockers.

'Take us to Winter Wonderland!'

Jack yelled on the third rock.

Chapter
Two

A few seconds later Jessica could feel an icy wind nipping at her cheeks. Snowflakes were swirling all around them.

Jack burst out laughing. 'Well, you wanted snow, Jessica. Now you've

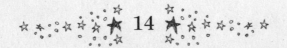

got it,' he said. 'This is *definitely* Winter Wonderland.'

'It's so pretty!' Jessica said, as they got up to look around. They were in the middle of a vast, snow-covered plain with a thicket of tall, dark green pine trees to their left.

As usual, the wishing-chair had disguised itself to fit in with its

surroundings.

It was now

a beautiful,

curved sleigh made of polished

oak with shiny silver runners, and

decorated with rows of tiny bells.

'Isn't it clever?' Jessica said. Then

something else caught her eye. 'Have

you noticed what we're all wearing?'

Jack's dressing-gown and slippers had vanished, and he was wearing a thick, woollen winter coat and sturdy boots. Jessica was dressed warmly, too, and even Wishler had a bulky green jacket and boots.

'It must be the magic of Winter Wonderland,' Wishler explained. 'To make sure we don't freeze –'

 17

'Listen!' Jack interrupted, putting his finger to his lips. 'Can you hear something?'

'It sounds like bells tinkling,' said

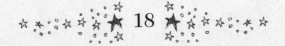

Jessica. 'And it's coming closer.'

Suddenly a group of twelve reindeer galloped out of the thicket of pine trees. They were bound together by a red harness decorated with bells, but they weren't pulling anything behind them. Three stern-faced elves dressed in green were riding on the reindeer at the front, urging them

to go faster.

'Those elves are Santa's helpers.'

Wishler explained.

Just then the elves spotted them.

They drew the reindeer to a swift halt and stared crossly at the three friends.

'Where *have* you been?' the biggest elf asked loudly. 'We've been waiting for you for *ages*!'

Jack and Jessica stared at them in amazement. They'd only just met Santa's elves, and it looked like they were already in trouble.

Chapter
Three

'This *is* the new sleigh that Santa ordered, isn't it?' the biggest elf went on, pointing to the wishing-chair. 'He needs it to make his Christmas deliveries – tonight!'

Before Jack, Jessica or Wishler

could say anything, all three elves jumped down from the reindeer.

'Actually, I don't think –' Wishler began hurriedly, but the elves weren't listening.

'Santa ordered this sleigh *weeks* ago,' the smallest elf complained.

'Um –' Wishler began again, but this time Jack cut him off.

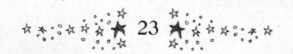

'Yes, we're sorry for the delay,' Jack said to the elves. Then he whispered to Jessica and Wishler: 'If we loan the sleigh to the elves to help them out, we might get to meet Santa!'

Jessica nodded. 'Good plan! And the *real* sleigh is bound to turn up soon,' she whispered back.

The elves had begun hitching the

reindeer's red harness to the sleigh.

'We should come, too,' Wishler said to them quickly, as the biggest elf picked up the reins. 'I'm Wishler and this is Jack and Jessica.'

'We can help make sure Santa's delivery goes smoothly,' Jack added.

The biggest elf nodded. 'OK, all of you climb aboard,' he said. 'I'm

Coney, the chief elf.'

'Hello, Coney,' Jack, Jessica and Wishler said together, but before they could say any more, Coney had shaken the reins and the sleigh shot off across the snow.

'This is awesome!' Jack yelled as the reindeer picked up speed and galloped across the snowy plain.

They passed the thicket of pine
trees, their branches dusted with
snow, and whizzed on. A little while
later they came to a large, frozen

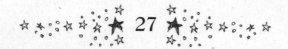

pond, glittering in the pale light.

'Look!' Jack nudged Jessica and pointed just ahead of them. Jessica saw a big wooden sign with *Santa's Christmas Workshop* painted in swirling red letters. The sign was in front of an enormous log cabin, the roof covered in thick snow and hung with twinkling white fairy lights.

As they got nearer, the tall wooden doors at the front of the cabin swung open and the sleigh sailed inside Santa's workshop. Jessica, Jack and

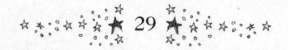

Wishler clapped their hands to their mouths in amazement. They'd never seen anything like *this* before!

Everywhere they looked, they could see towering piles of presents: dolls, jigsaws, board games, teddy-bears, gadgets, books and much, much more. There were hundreds of elves scurrying around busily.

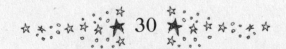

Some of them were putting gifts into bags and then ticking them off long lists. Others were bringing more presents and adding them to the heaps. A wonderful smell of gingerbread hung in the air.

'It's all go tonight!' Coney grinned as he guided the sleigh through the piles of toys. 'This is our Present

Workshop, and it's the biggest room we've got. It's where the elves collect all the presents that Santa has to deliver.'

'Look, Jessica,' said Jack, pointing at the wall ahead of them, his eyes wide.

Jessica saw a huge, wooden, red and white advent calendar on the

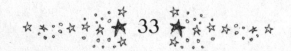

wall. The calendar had twenty-four silver doors, and twenty-three of them stood open, each revealing a sparkling frosted white snowflake that spun around.

'The last door to be opened is always the most spectacular and the one with the most Christmas spirit,' said Coney. 'It's tradition that Santa opens the door just before he sets off on Christmas Eve.'

'I hope we get to see that!' Jack exclaimed.

'Now I'll show you our Wrapping Room,' Coney went on, steering them round a corner. 'All of the

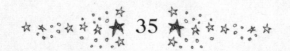

presents get wrapped here and loaded into the sleigh.'

'I hope Santa's real sleigh arrives in time,' Wishler whispered to Jack. 'Otherwise he'll need this one, and then how will we get home?'

'Let's worry about that later,' Jack said. 'We have to meet Santa!'

'We have the biggest conveyor belt

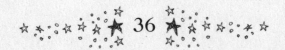

in the world,' Coney was saying. 'And lots of mechanical arms to help with the wrapping. You'll see the machine at full speed now, because Santa will be leaving soon –'

But when they stopped in front of the conveyor belt, it was chaos. The machine was jammed with presents and wasn't moving. The mechanical

arms weren't doing any wrapping,
either. Instead, there were sky-high
piles of glittery wrapping-paper and
shiny bows everywhere. Groups of

elves were frantically wrapping up
presents by hand.

Something was obviously very
wrong.

'Oh, Coney!' cried
a tiny blonde elf
running towards
them, tears streaming
down her face.

'The wrapping machine has jammed.
We've got thousands of presents to
wrap, and hardly any time left!'

'Don't worry, Snowy,' Coney said,
jumping down from the sleigh. 'I'll
fix it.'

Jack, Jessica and Wishler followed
Coney over to the huge machine.
Straightaway Jessica noticed sticky

golden-brown goo oozing out and dripping on to the floor.

'What's *that*?' she asked.

Coney bent to look. He sniffed the goo, and then stood up and removed a metal panel. He shone a torch into the machine and they could all see more of the sticky stuff clinging to the cogs and pistons inside.

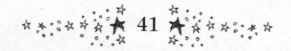

Coney drew back in shock. 'It's
full of toffee!' he announced.
'This machine has been jammed
deliberately!'

Chapter
Four

Everyone was horrified.

'Who would do this?' Snowy gasped.

'And on Christmas Eve too!'

'I don't know, but we have to get every scrap of toffee out right away,' Coney said grimly.

'We'll help,' Jack offered.

Snowy fetched some overalls for Jack, Jessica and Wishler, and also gave them a pile of cloths and some large spoons. Quickly, Jessica and Wishler began scooping out the toffee that had collected in the bottom of the machine, while Snowy, Jack and Coney tried to clean the workings.

 44

'The toffee is all squidgy because it got hot inside the machine,' Jack said, as he tried to wipe it off one of

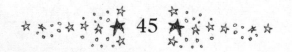

the pistons. The toffee clung to the cloth and to his fingers, and the more Jack tried to pull it off, the more it stuck. 'Yuk!' Jack dodged a soft, squashy lump of toffee as it dripped down, just missing his nose. 'What a waste of good toffee!'

'I don't think I ever want to eat toffee again,' Jessica groaned when

the insides of the machine were clean and shiny and silver again. Everyone had sticky goo in their hair and all over their clothes.

'Let's hope this works,' Coney said.

Everyone watched as he pressed a big red button on the side of the machine. There was a whirring sound

and suddenly the conveyor belt jolted into action. Jack, Jessica, Wishler and the elves cheered as the mechanical arms started to move.

The arms began reaching down to wrap presents neatly in glittering paper, adding a shiny bow on top.

'Oh, thank you, Coney!' Snowy said. 'And your new friends, too.'

Coney turned to Jack, Jessica and Wishler. 'She's right. We have a lot to thank you for. And I know just the thing to show our appreciation.'

49

'Can we meet Santa?' Jack asked.

Coney shook his head. 'You *might* catch a glimpse of him later, but we really can't disturb him this close to Christmas,' he replied. 'But I've got something fun for you to try. Follow me!'

Chapter
Five

Coney ushered Jack, Jessica and Wishler outside into the frosty air, grabbing three small boxes on the way. It was getting dark, but the fairy lights strung around the workshop lit everything up.

'I'm going to show you the latest elf craze – rocket skates!' Coney said, handing each of them a box.

'Cool!' Jack exclaimed, opening his up. The white boots had flashes of gold on the sides, and shiny silver blades. 'They look a bit like ice skates.'

'But the blades are much longer,'
Jessica pointed out.

'Which makes these skates super
fast,' Coney smiled. 'That's why they're
called *rocket* skates. Try them out!'

Quickly Jack, Wishler and Jessica
strapped the skates on. Jack was
ready first and set off across the
frozen pond.

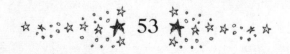

'Jack!' Jessica yelled. 'There are coloured sparks coming from your skates.'

Jack glanced behind him and saw silver sparks whirling from his blades. As he speeded up a little, the sparks changed colour, turning red, then purple, then blue.

'Hey, this is fun!' Jack shouted.

Wishler performed a wobbly figure of eight and was rewarded with a shower of green sparks. Jack and

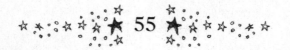
55

Jessica applauded. Then Jessica began to skate neatly backwards, sending pink sparks shooting in all directions.

'Let's have a race to the other side of the pond,' Jack shouted. 'Ready, steady –'

Suddenly a bell clanged.

'Oh no,' said Coney. 'That's the

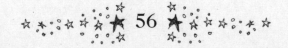

alarm!' The next moment the doors
of the workshop swung open, and a
big group of elves poured out.

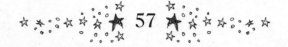

'Coney!' shouted Snowy. 'All the reindeer have gone missing!'

'There they are,' Jessica shouted. She pointed across the pond at the snowy plain. The reindeer were bolting down a slope away from the workshop.

'We've got no chance of catching them,' Coney said. Then he pointed

at Jessica, Jack and Wishler. 'But *you* have. Those rocket skates work on snow as well as ice.'

'After them!' Jack said to Jessica and Wishler.

The three friends chased after the reindeer in a shower of rainbow-coloured sparks.

Chapter
Six

They reached the other side of the
pond and whizzed off the ice on to
the snow.

'This is brilliant,' Jack yelled as
they skimmed across the surface
of the snow. 'It's like being on skis,

but ten times faster.'

Jack, Jessica and Wishler raced after the reindeer at high speed. Jessica took a quick look back over her shoulder, and saw that they were leaving a trail of fiery golden sparks behind them. She could also see Coney and the other elves chasing after them in the distance.

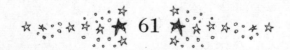

'We're catching up,' Jack shouted

as the reindeer flew past the thicket

of pine trees. 'These skates really *are*

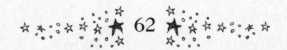

super fast!'

'But how do we get the reindeer to stop?' Jessica asked.

'I have an idea,' Wishler panted. 'But I'll have to use my own magic. I hope I can remember the spell.'

Wishler mumbled a few words under his breath and then snapped his fingers. To Jack and Jessica's

astonishment, bunches of carrots appeared in their hands.

'Reindeer love carrots,' Wishler called. He also had a bunch of them in each hand. 'I'm sure they'll stop when they see these.'

Jack, Jessica and Wishler managed to zoom past the reindeer. When they saw the carrots, the reindeer

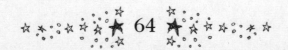

skidded to a halt, sending snow flying in all directions.

Jessica laughed. 'We did it!' She patted the reindeer nearest her and fed it a carrot. 'Well done, Wishler.'

'I'm just glad my magic worked,' Wishler said, as he and Jack gave carrots to all the other reindeer.

As the reindeer crunched away,

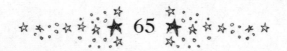

Coney and the other elves ran to join

them.

'Thank you,' Coney said, and the

 66

elves began to harness the reindeer together. 'It would have been terrible if they'd run off – Christmas would have been ruined!' Then he frowned. 'I wonder what frightened them away from the workshop.'

The elves led the reindeer back to their stable, and Jack, Jessica and Wishler skated back with Coney

walking alongside them. When they reached the Present Workshop again, the wishing-chair was waiting, ready to be loaded with presents.

'I have to help Santa prepare while the elves get the reindeer ready,' Coney told Jack, Jessica and Wishler. 'But you can help us load the presents on the sleigh, if you like.'

'Sounds great!' Jack said eagerly.

'Then we'll get to meet Santa.'

Coney grinned and hurried off.

'It doesn't look like the real sleigh

will arrive in time,' Jessica whispered, so that the two elves double-checking the presents couldn't hear.

'Well, it's OK if Santa uses our sleigh, isn't it?' Jack replied. 'I can't wait to meet him!'

'But remember what the Toymaker told us on our first wishing-chair adventure?' Jessica said. 'The chair can get impatient and make its own way home.'

'If that happens, Santa won't be able to deliver any presents *and* we'll be stranded in Winter Wonderland,' Wishler added.

'Hmm.' Jack looked worried. 'Maybe one of the elves can help us find out what's happened to the real sleigh.'

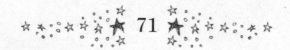

Jessica, Jack and Wishler went over to an elf who was frantically sifting through wish lists.

'Excuse me,' Jessica said. 'Please could you tell us where we might find the paperwork for the sleigh that Santa ordered?'

The elf looked up at them, frazzled. 'There!' he muttered. 'That scroll.'

He pointed to an enormous, golden scroll hanging on the wall. Jack, Jessica and Wishler hurried over to it.

'Placed orders,' Wishler read from the top of the scroll. There was a long list visible, but none of the entries was for Santa's sleigh.

'How will we find the order for the

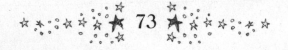

Santa's List

sleigh?' Jack wondered, sensing that

the elves didn't want to be disturbed.

'Luckily, I know how magic scrolls

work,' Wishler replied, his eyes twinkling. He touched the scroll lightly and said clearly, 'Sleigh!'

There was a flash of golden light, and the scroll began to roll on its own to a section called SANTA'S LIST.

Jessica began reading out the items:

1. A pair of xxl silk pyjamas ORDERED: 30th Sept DELIVERED: 10th Oct

2. 1 *Christmas Sleigh Deluxe* ORDERED: 15th Nov

   CANCELLED: 22nd Nov

3. 3 *lbs of Santa's Special Toffees* ORDERED: 24th Nov

   DELIVERED: 2nd Dec

'This makes no sense,' Jessica said, staring at Wishler and Jack in utter amazement. 'Santa cancelled his own sleigh!'

Chapter
Seven

'But why would he do that?' Jack asked, confused.

'I don't know,' Jessica said.

Just then, Coney came back into the Present Workshop, looking very miserable. Even his curled-up boots

seemed wilted.

'What's wrong?' asked Jessica.

'Santa is refusing to do the Christmas deliveries,' Coney said. 'None of us elves can convince him to change his mind. I don't know *what's* got into him.'

Suddenly Jack had an idea. He pointed to the list. 'Look!

Santa cancelled the sleigh,' he told Coney. 'And he must have ordered the toffee so that he could jam the wrapping machine. I just bet

he let the reindeer escape, too. All so that he could stop the Christmas deliveries.'

Coney looked shocked and sad. 'But Santa wouldn't do that. He *loves* Christmas.'

'Well, there's only one way to find out,' Jack said. 'I'm going to go and ask him –'

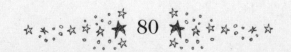

'Santa said he didn't want to be disturbed,' Coney said.

Jessica glanced at Jack. He looked very worried, but determined too. 'It doesn't matter what he said,' Jessica declared. 'This really is a Christmas emergency!'

Coney sighed. 'OK.'

He led them out of the Present

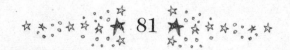

Workshop and down a hallway to a huge red door. Coney tapped on it and a deep voice inside called crossly, 'Come in.'

Jack, Jessica and Wishler followed Coney inside to see an enormous library. Its walls were lined with shelves stacked with old, leather-bound books. A roaring log fire burned in the grate, and standing at the window, looking out over the mountains of Winter Wonderland, was Santa himself!

Santa looked just like he did in all the pictures. He was very round and had rosy cheeks and a snowy beard. He wore a red and white suit and big black boots. But instead

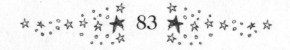

of a jolly smile, Santa looked very unhappy.

'We know about the toffee you ordered, and about the sleigh too,' Jack burst out. 'And we think you let the reindeer escape. But *why*?' Santa didn't answer. Instead he asked curiously, 'Who are you?'

'We're Jessica and Jack and we're

from Noware,' Jessica explained. Santa's bushy white eyebrows rose in surprise. 'And our friend Wishler is a pixie.'

'Our magical wishing-chair flew us here,' Jack explained, 'and then it disguised itself as a sleigh.'

'So that's how a sleigh arrived,' Santa said with a big sigh. 'You're

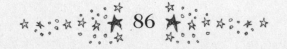 86

right. I did put toffee in the wrapping machine and I cancelled the sleigh.'

Coney gasped.

'But I did it for a good reason,' Santa went on.

'What reason?' Jessica wanted to know.

Santa looked like he was about to cry. 'I don't want to deliver presents

this Christmas because children don't believe in me any more.'

'That's not true,' Wishler said.

Santa opened his desk and drew out some sheets of paper. 'These charts show the numbers of people writing letters to Santa and visiting Santa's Grottos around the world,' he told them. He pointed at the chart.

'See how the numbers go down? People have stopped believing in me, and it's going to get worse.'

Santa stared miserably at Jack, Jessica and Wishler. 'Why should I go to the effort of delivering presents if no one believes in me?' he muttered. 'Children today don't need Santa, so I don't need them!'

Santa turned away from them and stared out of the window again.

Jack, Jessica and Wishler were

shocked. They never imagined Santa *not* delivering presents.

'We can't let this happen!' Jack said quietly.

'There'll be so many disappointed children if Santa doesn't change his mind,' Wishler agreed. 'But what can we do?'

Jessica racked her brains. 'We need

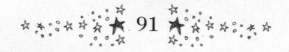

to show Santa how much Christmas cheer there is left in the world, to persuade him to give presents to the people who still believe in him.'

'Great idea,' Jack said. 'And I know just the thing.'

Jack stepped forward, slipped his hand into Santa's and began to pull him out of the room.

'Where are you taking me?' Santa said, surprised. 'I told you, I'm not going out tonight.'

'I want you to see something,' Jack said.

Jack led Santa, Jessica, Wishler and Coney down the corridor into the Present Workshop and stopped just in front of the advent calendar.

A little ladder had been placed just

below it.

'Even if you're not going to make

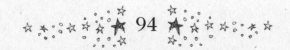 94

the deliveries, you have to open the last door on the advent calendar,' Jack insisted.

Jessica realised at once what Jack was doing. 'That's right!' she added, looking at all the anxious elves who were gathered round, watching. 'You have to open the door for all the elves who have worked so hard.'

Santa sighed. 'I'll do it, but I don't see what the point is.' He climbed up the ladder, looking down at his elves with a tear in his eye. Then he opened the shining silver door.

Jack and Jessica held their breath.

Chapter
Eight

There was a flash of white light and dazzling images began to pour out of the open door of the calendar. Jack and Jessica could hear beautiful music and the sound of children laughing with pleasure.

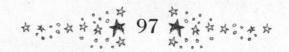

As Santa stood at the top of the ladder, glowing pictures surrounded him. Scenes of thousands of children all over the world writing letters to Santa and visiting Santa's Grottos. Some children were baking treats for Santa, as Jack and Jessica had done themselves, while others were wearing Santa suits for fancy-dress parties.

There were children opening presents under brightly-lit Christmas trees.

'I love you, Santa!' shouted a little girl as she unwrapped a parcel.

Jack, Jessica and Wishler gazed at Santa.

A happy smile spread across his face as the colourful images slowly faded away.

'How could I forget about all the boys and girls who *do* believe in me?' Santa thought aloud. 'No more dilly-dallying. We have millions of presents to deliver, and it's only a few hours till Christmas morning!'

Jack, Jessica and Wishler clapped their hands in delight, as Santa climbed down from the ladder and

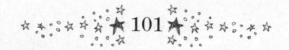

the elves began scurrying about in excitement.

'And it's all thanks to you,' Santa said to Jack. 'You've reminded me how much I love Christmas!'

'Christmas just wouldn't be the same without you,' Jack said, grinning.

Looking happy and full of new

energy, Santa gave Jack, Jessica and Wishler a hug. Then he turned to Coney, who was beaming from pointy ear to pointy ear. 'Coney, would you please get my sleigh out of the warehouse? It's not really broken. I'll be using that tonight!' Coney nodded and dashed away.

Santa explained to the friends,

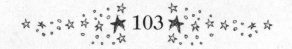

'Not that there's anything wrong with your wishing-chair, but I prefer my own sleigh.'

Jessica smiled, very relieved. 'Of course.'

All the elves rushed around preparing for Santa's departure. Jack, Jessica and Wishler joined in, helping them to pack all the

presents in the sleigh.

Soon everything was ready. The three friends stood on the steps in front of the workshop with Coney, Snowy and the other elves, under the cold night sky. They watched Santa climb into the battered old sleigh piled with presents. The reindeer had been harnessed to the sleigh, and

were pawing the ground impatiently, their breath steaming in the frosty air.

'Thank you, Jack, Jessica and Wishler, for showing me that people *do* still believe in me!' Santa called, waving at them. 'Thank you, Coney, and all of the elves for your hard work!'

The clock above the door of the

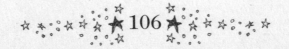

workshop began to chime, and all the elves cheered.

'It's midnight, and that means it's Christmas Day,' Jessica said happily. 'Merry Christmas, Santa!'

'Merry Christmas!' Santa called back, shaking the reins. The reindeer began to gallop across the snow and after a few moments they rose gracefully up

into the air. Everyone cheered again

as they waved Santa on his way.

Jessica grinned at Wishler and

Jack. Then, to her alarm, she noticed

that Wishler was flickering out of sight, as if he was disappearing.

'Look at Wishler!' Jessica nudged Jack. 'The chair's ready to go home.'

'Coney, we must go,' Jack said.

Coney frowned. 'OK, but I don't even know how you got here.'

'We'll show you,' Jessica said.

Jack, Jessica and Wishler rushed

over to the wishing-chair. Jessica
touched the sleigh and said, 'Show
yourself!' Coney, Snowy and the
other elves watched in amazement
as the wishing-chair appeared.

Then Coney smiled. 'Even if you
aren't the sleigh people, we're so glad
you came. And you're welcome to
come back anytime.'

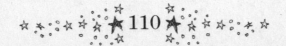

Waving goodbye, Jack, Jessica and Wishler sat down and began to rock.

'Home!' Jack called on the third rock as the elves shouted farewell.

There was a flash of blue light, and when it had faded, Jack, Jessica and Wishler found themselves back in the shed at the bottom of the garden.

'It's morning!' Jack gasped, looking through the window at the golden sky streaked with pale pink.

'And it's been snowing!' Jessica said with delight.

The three of them hurried out of the shed into the beautiful white-covered garden.

'Look,' Jessica pointed to some very large boot prints in the snow. They were surrounded by lots of smaller prints that looked like reindeer hooves.

'Santa's been,' Jack shouted in

delight as they saw a light go on in
their parents' bedroom.

'We have to go, Wishler,' Jessica
said. 'Merry Christmas!'

'Merry Christmas,' Wishler replied, hugging them both.

Wishler went into the shed and Jack and Jessica raced for the back door of the house.

'The wishing-chair has given us the best Christmas ever,' Jessica said.

'And it's only just begun,' Jack replied happily.

EGMONT PRESS: ETHICAL PUBLISHING

Egmont Press is about turning writers into successful authors and children into passionate readers – producing books that enrich and entertain. As a responsible children's publisher, we go even further, considering the world in which our consumers are growing up.

Safety First
Naturally, all of our books meet legal safety requirements. But we go further than this; every book with play value is tested to the highest standards – if it fails, it's back to the drawing-board.

Made Fairly
We are working to ensure that the workers involved in our supply chain – the people that make our books – are treated with fairness and respect.

Responsible Forestry
We are committed to ensuring all our papers come from environmentally and socially responsible forest sources.

For more information, please visit our website at www.egmont.co.uk/ethical

Egmont is passionate about helping to preserve the world's remaining ancient forests. We only use paper from legal and sustainable forest sources, so we know where every single tree comes from that goes into every paper that makes up every book.

This book is made from paper certified by the Forestry Stewardship Council (FSC), an organisation dedicated to promoting responsible management of forest resources. For more information on the FSC, please visit **www.fsc.org**. To learn more about Egmont's sustainable paper policy, please visit **www.egmont.co.uk/ethical**.